D0245251

Dedicated to my feisty young daughter, Pearl

Withdrawn from stock

Mr. and Mrs. Power
had a baby girl.
She was small and round
so they named her PEARL

PEARL POWER

Written and Illustrated by
Mel Elliott

Pearl

was anxious, Pearl was sad,
they were moving house,
and this could be bad.

Pearl tried to keep smiling,
they were moving because,
her Mum had been clever
and they'd made her the

BOSS

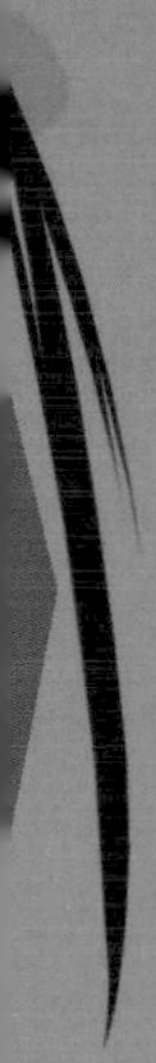

She

would miss her bedroom
and the kids on her street,

but she thought about all the cool
kids she might meet,

like kids who are shy and kids who are smart,
some great at science and some good at art.

As her mum loaded boxes onto the lorry,
she ruffled Pearl's hair and said not to worry.
"The time has come to leave this town,
life's a journey, don't you frown."

Pearl and her Mum drove off the next day,

with a stop for a burger along the way.

They talked of the great new life they would make

NEW HOUSE

(and also which junctions and exits to take).

The new house was bigger than the one before,
with a big shiny lion upon the front door,
and a big luscious garden with a swing in a tree.
Pearl smiled proudly "Yep this is for me!"

Monday came, there were butterflies in tummies.
Not just in Pearl's but also in Mummy's.
"Good luck" they said as they left at the gate,
Mum had to dash - the boss couldn't be late!

The new school was huge and Pearl was afraid,
but she had to be tough, it was time to be brave.
Most of the kids were bigger than Pearl,
but she knew that *she* was a clever strong girl.

When it was playtime they played with a ball,
and a boy named Sebastian who was ever so tall,
laughed "HAHAHA You throw like a girl!"
and she knew what to do, "Why thank you!" said Pearl.

"If you thought that was good
then get ready for this,"
and she held the ball
oh so tight in her fist.
"He can't squish me
like some dainty flower,
for I am Pearl,
and I have Pearl Power!"

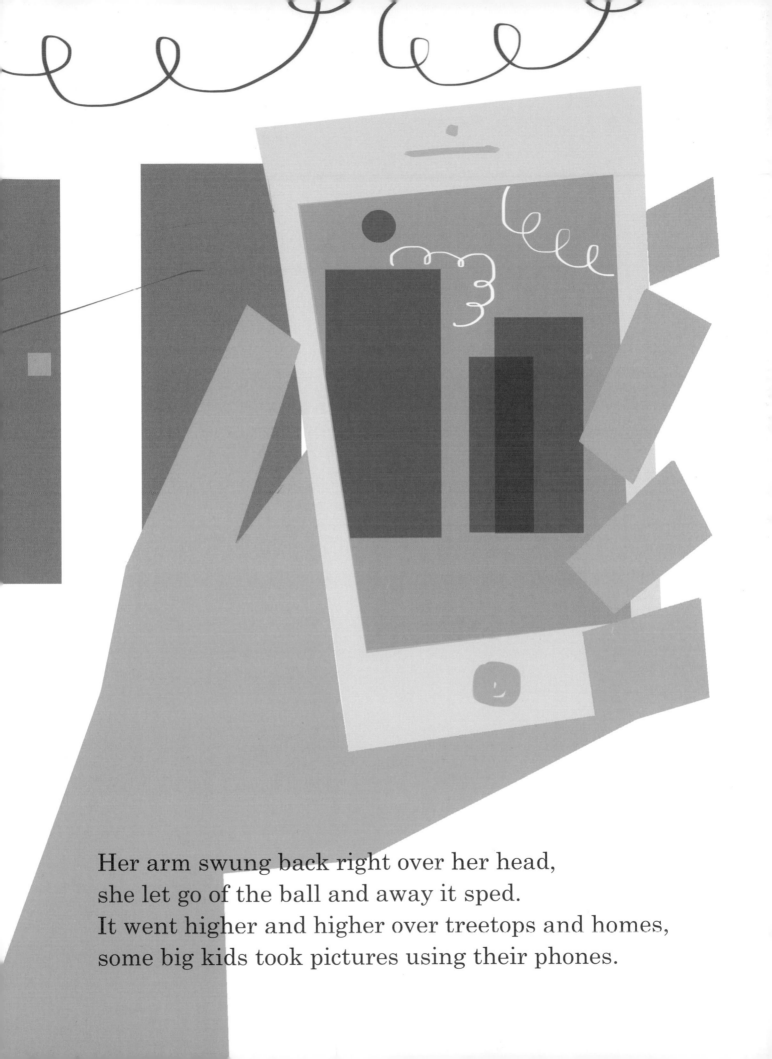

Her arm swung back right over her head,
she let go of the ball and away it sped.
It went higher and higher over treetops and homes,
some big kids took pictures using their phones.

Sebastian yelled "Will my ball be back soon?"
"Nah," said Pearl, "It's gone to the moon!"

After break it was time to do sums,
and the classroom was full of kids sat on their bums.
One by one they did their times table,
but when it came to Pearl's turn she was simply unable!

EMPTY

She didn't want to get her sums wrong,
but when she checked in her brain,
all the numbers had

GONE!

Sebastian laughed

You do maths
like a girl!

And she knew
what to do

Why
thank you!

said Pearl.

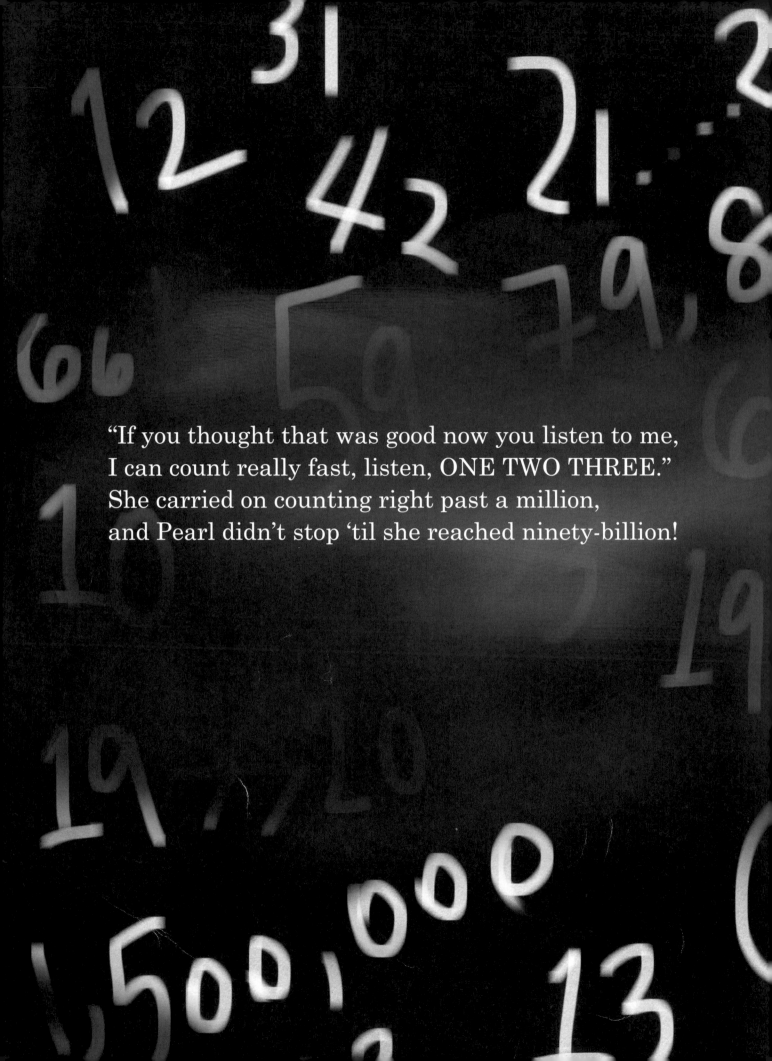

"If you thought that was good now you listen to me,
I can count really fast, listen, ONE TWO THREE."
She carried on counting right past a million,
and Pearl didn't stop 'til she reached ninety-billion!

"Don't laugh at me for getting things wrong,
for I am a girl who's clever and strong."
Sebastian frowned, "That's stupid" he snapped.
All the other kids cheered and clapped.

Now Pearl could always run really fast,
and when she raced she never came last.
but during PE they were running around
when Pearl tripped up and fell to the ground.

Sebastian laughed,
"HAH you run like a girl!"
She knew what to do,
"Why thank you!" said Pearl.

"If you thought that was fast,
well now watch me go,"
and she ran round the track
not the slightest bit slow.
She jumped over puddles
and though her knee was sore,
she ran so fast
that it hurt no more.

The school bell rang, it was time to go home,
but Sebastian was crying and all alone.
It was raining fast, he was getting all wet,

"Your mum is running late I'll bet?"

She gave him a **cuddle!**

"You hug like a girl," Sebastian said.

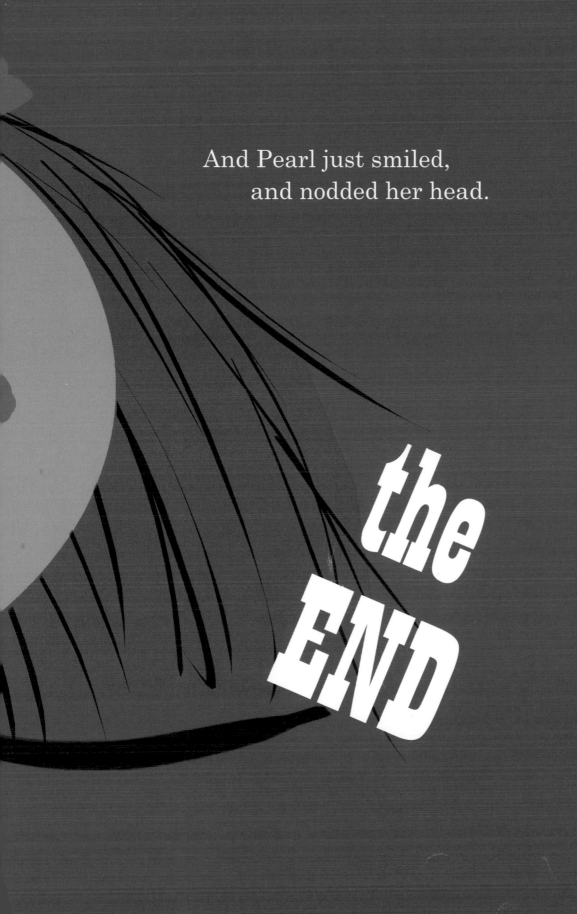

And Pearl just smiled,
and nodded her head.

the
END

First published in the United Kingdom by I LOVE MEL
6th Floor, Cavendish House
Hastings
East Sussex
TN34 3AA

I LOVE MEL is a trading name of Brolly Associates Ltd.

Copyright © Mel Elliott, 2014

All rights reserved. No part of this publication may be reproduced, stored in a retrieval system, or transmitted in any form or by and means electronic, mechanical, photocopying, recording or otherwise, without the prior written permission of the copyright owner.

ISBN 9780992854416

10 9 8 7 6 5 4 3 2

Printed by CMYK, LONDON.

This book can be ordered direct from the publisher at
www.ilovemel.me

Mel Elliott was born in Barnsley, UK and now lives and works in Hastings on the south coast. She is a graduate of The Royal College of Art, London.

Having spent several years illustrating and publishing grown-up, contemporary colouring books, Mel became inspired by her own daughter, Pearl and the frustrating issue of sexual stereotypes forced upon young children.

Pearl Power is Mel's first children's book and was developed primarily to tackle gender stereotypes. Pearl Power was published around the notion that the earlier little boys and girls learn about sexual equality, the better!